D1564930

Howling for Home

by Joan Carris

Illustrated by Judith Mitchell

Little, Brown and Company

Boston   Toronto   London

For Stephanie Owens Lurie, my editor —
thank goodness

First Edition

The characters and events in this book are fictitious. Any similarity to
real persons, living or dead, is coincidental and not intended by the
author.

Library of Congress Cataloging-in-Publication Data

Carris, Joan Davenport.
    Howling for home / by Joan Carris. — 1st ed.
      p. cm.
    Summary: Dissatisfied at having to eat dry food, sleep in
the laundry room, and wear a collar, Beau, a newly adopted
puppy, decides to run away.
    ISBN 0-316-13017-6
    1.   Dogs — Juvenile   fiction.   [1.   Dogs — Fiction]   I.   Title.
PZ10.3.C25Ho   1992
[E] — dc20   91-44852

Springboard books and design is a registered trademark of Little,
Brown and Company (Inc.)

10 9 8 7 6 5 4 3 2 1

WOR

Published simultaneously in Canada
by Little, Brown & Company (Canada) Limited

PRINTED IN THE UNITED STATES OF AMERICA

1

With joy the large puppy burst out of his travel crate. He was sick of bouncing and bumping in it from place to place.

"Oh, hey, he's cool! Here, boy!"

The puppy sniffed the small hand stretched toward him. He looked around and saw nothing familiar. For the first time in his life, he was inside a house.

The three new people all petted him at once. Then the boy tugged at his collar. "Here's Uncle Matt's note, Mom." Out loud, he read,

Howdy, folks.

Here's the pick of Gallant Lady's litter. He's six months now, housebroken, and smart as all get-out. I'll send a book on Bernese mountain dogs soon as I can.

You're going to love being dog owners. Just be firm and remember who's boss. His shots are up-to-date, but sign him up with a good vet right away, okay? Talk to you soon. Hugs all around.

Matt

P.S. The name on his papers is Gallant B . . .

Michael stopped reading. "What's this word, Dad?"

His father took the note. "It's Beau. You pronounce it 'bow,' like the bow on a present. Gallant Beau."

"What a dopey name." Michael frowned.

"It's perfect," Mom said. She was still petting him, and Beau's eyes closed in pleasure at her touch.

"Beau is an old French name," Dad explained. "It suggests a handsome sweetheart, a noble friend, a brave soldier —"

"That will do, dear," Mom said.

Beau listened to the people's voices and felt their excitement. It made him wriggle from head to tail.

He leapt up and down to show them how strong he was and how high he could jump. He was the only real jumper in his litter of eight.

"I think he needs to go out," said Dad.

Beau dashed out as soon as Michael opened the door. He wet two trees and a bush fast. He could tell that no dogs had been here.

He marked several more bushes with his special scent. Wanting to be thorough, he wet a tire on the car, too.

He kept looking for something familiar.

High peaks with snowy tops? Roads smelling of mud and tall firs that sighed with wind in their branches? Many dogs and men and cattle? Those were the things he knew.

Here was nothing he knew. He couldn't understand it. The strangeness of everything made him whimper.

Michael knelt beside him. "You miss home in Montana, hunh?"

The sound of the boy's voice and the kindness in his hands made Beau feel better. He licked Michael's ear and then his face, doing a careful job.

"I'll bet you're hungry," Michael said. "Be right back." He went inside and returned with a bowl. "Go on," he urged. "It's puppy chow."

Beau nosed the puppy chow. He crunched a few dry bites. At home, his food dripped with tasty gravy. It was always nice and soft.

This food was hard and noisy. It made his ears angry. He left the bowl to mark three

more trees and another car tire. He liked being busy. Just now he was in the mood for a cat.

But there was no cat, or anything else that he knew. He flopped onto the grass, nose on his paws.

Michael began talking to him and stroking him again. For a time, Beau forgot about home.

When night came, Dad put him in his crate. Beau pawed at the latch on the crate and barked.

"Sssh," Dad said. "It's nice and warm here in the laundry room. Curl up on that old towel and sleep." He left the little room and shut the door.

Beau heard steps going away. His nose had begun to itch and he sneezed several times.

And now he was in his crate again, alone, as he had been most of the day.

It was all too much. Beau threw his head back and howled.

2

For some time, Beau howled.

When no one came, he tried to dig or chew out of his crate. The wire mesh tasted simply awful.

All along, his nose burned and itched. Something in this little room was very bad for dogs. He sneezed until his head stuffed up. "Aaoooooooo," he mourned.

And finally, the people came.

"He's homesick," Michael said, looking in at Beau. "His nose and eyes are runny, too."

"Matt said to be firm," Mom reminded

them. "A dog cannot make the rules."

"He's only a puppy!" cried Michael. "He's lonely!"

Dad nodded. "Okay. I hate being firm at midnight. Take him outdoors and then he can stay in your room."

Soon, Beau was curled up on Michael's bed. The smells there were much nicer. It wasn't the same as his mother and his litter-mates, but he was comforted.

Breakfast the next morning was more puppy chow. It was tasteless and noisy, but Beau was terribly hungry.

He washed it down with a drink from the toilet and went outdoors with Michael.

Too soon, Dad came outside. He put Beau back in his crate in the laundry room. "Sorry, fella, but we're gone all day and this is your place."

His nose began to sting right away and he

sneezed. Misery washed over him, making him howl again. Now and then he added a long, sad whimper.

Once more the people came. Michael whispered to him through the wire mesh.

Mom and Dad bent over his crate. "So far," Mom said, "I do *not* love being a dog owner. What do you think Matt knows about dogs that we don't?"

"Everything," Dad replied.

Mom took her keys out of her purse. "I have to get to work, you guys. Let's try leaving him in the kitchen with the doors shut. And don't forget his water."

All that day, Beau slept on the soft rug in front of the sink. He was still tired from his long trip the day before.

After school, he and Michael went outside and rolled in the grass with a boy named Greg. The two boys threw sticks for him to chase — a new game for Beau.

It wasn't as much fun as a cat, of course. Still, he loved leaping up to catch the stick.

He was chewing one when he heard Michael holler, "Oww!" Instantly he dropped the stick and ran to Michael.

"Hrrrr," he growled at the other boy. It wasn't as big a growl as he wanted, so he bared his teeth.

"Whoa," Greg said, backing away.

Mom came outdoors on the run.

"We were just wrestling. For fun," Greg explained. "Does he bite?"

"He's not supposed to," Mom replied, shaking her head.

"I know what happened," said Michael. "Beau was guarding me! I yelled really loud when we were wrestling."

"I see." Mom nodded. "Look," she went on, "I bought a leash today. Why don't you all go for a walk?"

Beau trotted along on the sidewalk, but something was wrong. He moved to the grass and that felt more normal.

"Ssssss!" he heard from behind a hedge.

So. There *were* cats here! Beau took off, joy in his heart.

Michael hauled back on the leash and shouted, "No!"

Aarr! The collar made him gag and choke. Worse yet, the fat white cat was teasing him and getting away with it.

Wildly, he flung himself at her.

But the boys were stronger than he, and they dragged him back into the Owens' yard.

Greg scowled. "He doesn't do anything right."

"He does, too!" flared Michael. "He's just new!"

Beau lay in the grass, his neck hurting. The little bit of joy was gone, so soon. What kind of place was this?

3

For the next two days, Beau ate little and slept poorly. In dreams he was home — chasing his littermates across the open land. He whimpered in his sleep, and his paws scrabbled at the bedcovers.

Early one evening, Dad put him with Michael in the front seat of the car. "I'll manage Beau tonight," Dad said. "It's tricky taking a dog to the vet."

"How?" asked Michael.

"You'll see," Dad said.

Beau had been in a car only twice before,

but he had ridden in his crate. This time he could stick his head out the window. His nose tingled with new odors and he loved the feel of wind on his face.

In the vet's parking lot, Dad took his leash.

Beau stopped short. Bad smells were drifting his way: medicine and disinfectant and fear. He remembered from early puppyhood.

"Beau?" Dad asked politely. "Come on."

Finally, Dad picked him up and lugged him into the vet's office. Michael followed, smiling.

"Rats," Dad said as he signed the register. "Lots of folks are ahead of us."

Now that he was inside, Beau got excited. *Dogs.* All kinds of dogs.

And cats! He stuck his nose in the cage of a sleek Siamese, who went crazy. She arched her back and hissed and let out piercing yowls.

Beau was pleased. It was more than he had hoped for.

In the near corner was a young Shetland sheepdog female. He put his nose on her tender one.

He greeted a collie pup next, then an old beagle.

Dad turned to leave the desk and nearly fell down.

Michael pointed to Dad's ankles. Beau's leash was wrapped around them several times.

People in the waiting room giggled and pointed.

It was some time before the leash could be unwound and even longer before the red went out of Dad's face.

When their name was called, they all went into the examining room.

Dr. Sushito's smile was broad. "You lucky people," she said. "A Bernese mountain dog. Where'd you get him?" She hugged Beau and rubbed noses with him.

Beau's hazel eyes stared into her dark eyes

and he liked her. She smelled good, almost like another dog.

Her hands felt him all over — knowing, gentle hands. To Dad she said, "And how does he like our city suburbs?"

"He doesn't, I'm afraid. He's jumpy, he won't eat, and he won't go properly for walks."

"You must learn to think like this dog," Dr. Sushito said. "His breed likes to work, you know. They're born to guard homesteads or cattle — or people, for that matter. They're a fine breed, but not common here on the East Coast. How did you happen to get one?"

"My wife's brother in Montana raises them — the smaller, original Bernese from Switzerland. He says they're the best."

The vet nodded. "Yes, but he'll need real jobs — just as retrievers and shepherds do. What are you teaching him? And are you going to the park for long runs?"

Dad was silent. He was turning red again.

Suddenly the vet smiled. "We'll fix all of you, don't worry. Now let's talk about his diet and his lessons."

Later, Beau licked Dr. Sushito goodbye. He trotted gladly back to the car.

All the way home he held his head out the window so that the wind would ripple his ears. His nose sorted out all the interesting smells.

That's how he caught various food odors in the air. They made his stomach knot with hunger.

4

"Mmnn," Beau whimpered. His tongue dripped saliva as he sniffed the good smell. He sat right at Mom's feet.

Soon, she set a dish on the floor and said, "Go to it."

It was his then! Beau nearly choked on the first hungry bite. Not what he was used to, but good. Yes, awfully good. He wolfed the rest of it.

He licked the bowl repeatedly, seeking every morsel. After a fresh drink from the toilet, he went back to the kitchen and licked Mom's hand.

"Why does he drink from the toilet when we set water out for him?" Mom asked. She wiped her soggy hand on her slacks.

"All dogs do that," Michael said, laughing.

"He drips water all over the seat," she said. "But he liked the vet's recipe and now he's eating. I guess I should be grateful." She nuzzled Beau's head and he licked her ear.

Beau and Michael went out to play in the darkening yard then. They didn't come in until homework time.

Because Michael was reading, Beau looked for Dad. Dad was making banging noises in the basement. "Stay out of the sawdust," Dad said.

Mom was busy, too, although she hugged him and said, "Good dog," when he put his head on her knee.

Bored, Beau lay down on a rug by the laundry room. He had a happy stomach for the first time in days and he felt like action.

He caught a whiff of the nasty smell in the laundry room. Of course. There was work to be done.

He nosed open the laundry room door and sneezed violently. Nothing had ever hurt his nose like this. He knew now what it was, too.

Beau fixed his eyes on the box of soap powder. He stood up on his hind legs and stretched. He could just barely get his mouth around the box.

Errrchew! The box went flying. It bounced off the washing machine and onto the floor.

Nose smarting, Beau took the box in his teeth and carried it to a heap of clothes in the corner.

He wormed around until the soap was on the very bottom of the heap. It made his nose burn, but it was worth it. Now the bad box was well chewed and well buried.

He celebrated with a nice long drink of water.

And still there was nothing to do. He would have chewed his new rawhide bone, but he couldn't find it.

Through the open laundry room door he spotted the dust mop. He had seen Mom shake it hard. It must be bad, and that's why it needed shaking.

Well, then. She had given him a most tasty meal. He would do something for her.

Beau took the mop to the middle of the laundry room and gave it a good shake. Dust flew and again he sneezed. He shook it some more. It made his nose itch horribly.

Now he was mad at the mop. He lay down on the floor and began to chew its handle. His sharp new teeth cut easily into the soft wood. Soon, the mop was in two pieces.

He stood up and looked down at the pieces. He pawed the mop head that had come off its handle. He felt sure the mop was dead. It was a good feeling.

He looked around for more work and saw

the vacuum in the corner. Michael had kicked it when he had to vacuum his room. It must be bad, too. He knew Michael hated it.

The vacuum gave him more trouble than the mop. He couldn't chew the metal parts. They hurt his teeth.

But he could and did chew the rubber bumper all around the metal housing. He turned it into dozens of tiny, wet pieces.

There. That would hold the vacuum for a while. It wasn't dead like the mop, but it was the best he could do.

Beau viewed the laundry room with pride. He had fixed all the problems in here that he could think of.

5

Beau was upstairs with Michael when he heard Mom's angry voice. The whole family met at the laundry room door.

Michael took one look and grabbed Beau's collar. "Don't go in there," he warned.

"It's a bit late now, isn't it?" Mom snapped. "Why in heaven's name would he make such a mess?"

Dad took Mom's arm. "I expect he just got bored. Come into the kitchen, Janey, and relax. We'll clean it up."

"Dad's right, Mom," said Michael. "The vet said he needs jobs to do and lots of exercise."

Mom made a face. "Jobs? Such as fetching slippers and the newspaper? Somehow, I don't think that's going to do it. He must love to chew. Where's his rawhide bone anyway?"

Beau sank lower and lower until he was flat on the floor. They were very mad at him. And after all his careful work, too. It was confusing.

"Let's clean up," Dad said to Michael.

Mom punched telephone buttons. "Hello, Matt? Boy, am I glad you're home! Beau's tying us in knots here. Let me tell you what he just did."

Beau slunk under the table.

Much later Mom said, "Okay, I'll watch for the book. But if you don't quit laughing, we're taking you off our Christmas list forever!"

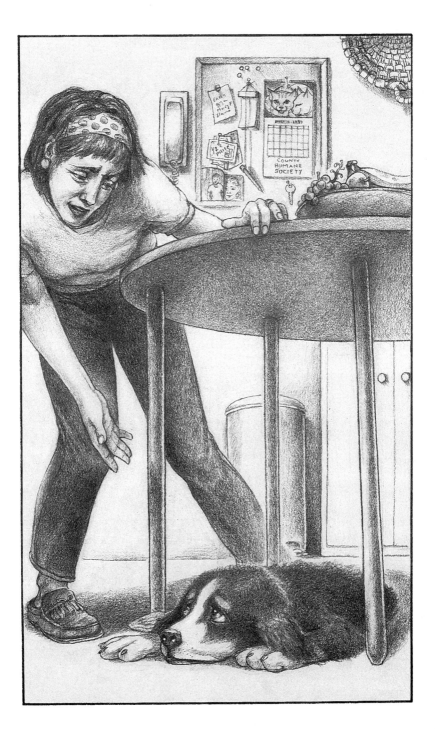

She hung up the phone and peered under the table.

Beau looked into her eyes. She was done yelling. He crawled out from under the table and sat beside her. He put his head on her knee and gazed right at her face.

"Beau," she said softly, "you are a pill. A very, very lovable pill." She began to stroke his head.

He closed his eyes in pleasure. His mother had always licked his head and it felt much like this.

"Beau," Mom went on, "I don't know about dogs. You're my very first puppy."

He scooched closer to her body.

"Somehow," she said, "we have to do this right."

"I know how!" Michael called from the laundry room.

"Me too," said Dad, popping into the kitchen. "The vet said obedience training was a must."

Michael joined them in the kitchen. He was holding the box of soap. "Looks like he chewed it a lot. Then he hid it under the dirty clothes. Isn't that funny, you guys?"

"It does have a certain charm," Mom replied.

"Hrrrrr," Beau growled, his eyes on the bad box. Why had they dug it up after he had so carefully buried it?

"Aha!" Dad said. "Light is dawning. He really hates that soap. Look at his bared teeth."

Just then Beau sneezed. And sneezed again.

"I bet it hurts his nose," Michael said. "Dogs have noses you wouldn't believe."

Michael got down on his knees and put his arms around Beau. "We're sure dumb, huh?"

"Okay, okay," Mom said. "You win, guys. One course at obedience school, coming right up."

"I get to take him," Michael said. "He's my dog."

* * *

Several days later, Dad drove Michael and Beau to the high school after dinner. "Obedience classes meet in the gym," Dad said. "I'll be waiting here after class."

Even before the car drove away, Beau heard dogs. With a glad heart, he leapt forward.

"Slow down!" Michael hollered all the way into the gym.

The teacher came swiftly toward them. "You must be Michael," she said. "I'm Mrs. Frank. I told your mother I don't approve of young dog handlers. If you cannot control your dog, you'll have to leave."

Aaarr! Beau choked as Michael hauled him up short. "I'll control him," Michael said.

Beau shook his head and neck until they felt normal again. Which dog should he greet first?

Then he saw her — the Shetland sheepdog he had met at the vet's. He took off running.

6

On his way to the sheltie, Beau dragged Michael past a shining black Labrador, a standard gray poodle, and a golden retriever.

"Rowf," greeted the big retriever.

Mrs. Frank hurried after Beau and Michael. "I'll help you put on his training collar," she told Michael.

The new collar was noisy as its chain links slid past Beau's ears. Still, he could hardly feel it on his neck.

"Pull toward you on the leash," the teacher told Michael. "The chain will rattle in his ears and the collar will get tighter. He'll soon learn to do as you say."

"I'll bet," Michael said in a small voice. He bent down to hug Beau. "Don't be stubborn, okay?" he whispered.

Just then a bushy-tailed Pomeranian dashed up to them.

Beau curled his lip at the barking, leaping pom. Bushy-tails were just pests, and too small to be of any real use.

The pom's owner said, "I'm Mrs. Portly and this is Prudy. Say hello, Prudy, sweetheart."

"Yap, yap, yap!" sassed Prudy.

Beau lunged at little Bushy-Tail.

"No!" cried Michael, pulling back on the leash.

The collar rattled nastily in Beau's ears. It pressed in on his throat. He sat down to paw at the awful thing.

Michael urged him across the room, away from the pom. They ended up beside the Shetland sheepdog and her owner, a teenage girl.

"I'm Debbie," the girl said. "My sheltie is Dinah. We saw you at the vet's, remember?"

Beau once again touched noses with the lovely Dinah.

Mrs. Frank clapped her hands. "Okay, everyone. Dogs on your left. Walk slowly in a circle around the gym."

Seven dogs and seven people walked, jerked, or leapt forward. Just ahead of Beau was Rex, a miniature Doberman. He was small and sleek and nervous. Every few feet he turned and snarled.

Beau didn't like it. He waited, and the next time Rex turned around, Beau sprang forward.

Aaarr! Tight, tighter around his throat. *Rattle-rattle* in his ears. He froze and the collar grew quiet.

Michael turned to Debbie behind him. "Some of these dogs are a real pain. How's Dinah doing?"

"Okay," Debbie replied, "I'm keeping her away from Rex and Prudy."

"Good idea," agreed Michael. "Come on, Beau. We're holding up the whole class."

Beau set out again, on Michael's left, with extreme caution. Now he couldn't even feel the bad collar.

The teacher called, "Stop, everyone. We must learn the command 'Heel.' Step out with your left foot first.

"If your dog gets ahead of you, make a sharp right turn so he has to run to catch up. Say his name, then 'Heel!' Praise him as soon as he's walking beside you. Okay, go."

The class walked briefly. Then the people made sharp right turns. They walked a few steps, names rang out, and more sharp right turns were made. They were all over the place, in no set pattern.

"Sorry," Michael said as he whammed into Mrs. Portly.

"Yap, yap!" scolded Prudy, nipping at

34

Beau's heels.

That did it. Beau went for Prudy's tail, but Michael's hands clamped his jaws shut.

"No, no! If we fight, we get kicked out."

Beau wriggled with anger. That sassy-tailed dog needed a good lesson — from *him*.

Michael urged him into place and they went on practicing the command "heel." It wasn't any fun. Just as he was sailing along, his ears lifting in the air . . . *yank*.

"Beau, heel!" Michael ordered.

Once more the collar rattled and tightened around his throat. Mad at the noise and the choking feeling, he stopped fast. The collar settled softly on his neck.

Suddenly he understood. If he stopped pulling away, the bad collar couldn't get him.

The next time Michael said, "Beau, heel," he stopped pulling forward immediately. The collar didn't press in on his throat and it didn't make a sound.

"Good dog!" cried Michael. "What a great

dog!" he petted him over and over, repeating, "Good dog."

Beau wagged his whole body and whimpered with joy.

Michael stood up. "Beau, heel," he said.

Together they moved forward. Beau stayed next to Michael's leg. He had to make the collar behave itself.

Michael turned right. He pulled gently on the leash and the collar tightened a teeny bit.

Beau hurried to catch up. He stayed close to Michael's leg, where it was safe.

And again Michael said, "Good dog!"

Beau's head lifted and he stepped out proudly. This was a very sneaky collar, but he had figured it out. He had made it mind him.

He found he could look around now at the other dogs. He didn't have to think of the collar every minute.

Instead, he looked for little Bushy-Tail. He wasn't finished with her yet.

7

At home, Michael told his parents about the first class. "Beau heeled the best."

Beau heard the word *heel* and remembered what it meant. No following your nose to where it led. No running as the air streamed past your head.

He had always run free, until recently. Life had been very different . . . before.

Here, he was the only dog, not one of many. He slept on the boy's bed, not with his mother in the barn. He played chase-the-stick and tug-of-war with a long sock — new games. Still, he remembered the old life.

Every day he and Michael practiced heeling.

New smells drew him on as they walked. Naturally, he set out to investigate them.

"Beau, heel," Michael would say. And . . . *yank*.

Disgusted — fed up with the sneaky collar — he heeled.

He learned to keep his shoulders in line with the boy's body. Michael gave him Chewy-Chockos, dog candy.

After a week, they were ready for the second class. As soon as they entered the gym, Prudy started in. "Yap, yap, yap!"

Beau lunged forward, but Michael pulled back hard.

The teacher spoke to Mrs. Portly. "Keep Prudy quiet, please. She must not annoy other dogs."

Michael made sure Beau's collar had

loosened. "Good dog, good dog!" he repeated.

Beau hardly heard him. His eyes followed rude little Bushy-Tail.

"Okay, folks, show me how to walk a dog," said Mrs. Frank, smiling at the class.

Debbie and the ladylike Dinah were in front of Beau and Michael when they lined up. The Doberman Rex and Mrs. Rand were behind them.

After one calm circle around the gym, Rex began sneaking forward for quick sniffs of Beau's tail.

Beau spun around and snapped his teeth in Rex's face.

"Bad dog!" Mrs. Rand shouted at Beau.

"Hey!" Michael said. "It was Rex who —"

"No fighting," the teacher called out. "Keep your dogs under control at all times."

Beau was held tight against Michael's body. He could only bare his teeth. He tried to show lots of teeth.

Rex snarled back.

Michael moved Beau next to Dinah and Debbie. "Geez," he said to Debbie, "Rex and Prudy keep getting us in trouble. All the other dogs are real nice."

Debbie nodded. "Yeah, but Rex and Prudy's owners don't know what they're doing. Just stay near us, okay?"

Beau sniffed Dinah and licked her head. He forgot all about Rex and Bushy-Tail.

Mrs. Frank clapped her hands. "Okay, people. The next command is 'Sit.' I will demonstrate with our Bernese."

First, she petted Beau. Then she took his leash in hand and raised up on it. "Beau, sit," she said as she pressed down on his rump. Naturally, he sat.

"Good dog!" she cheered, petting him some more.

The collar loosened and Beau stood up. Now was no time to sit. Rex was inching closer. "Hrr," he warned.

Quickly, the teacher moved between the dogs. "These two really don't like each other," she said. "Mrs. Rand, please take Rex to the other side of the gym."

Everyone began practicing the new command.

"Beau, sit."

Beau felt his head being pulled up as his rump was pushed down, just like before. He sat. When the collar felt okay, he stood up again.

"Rowf, ROWF!" barked the golden retriever and the black Labrador. Neither dog wanted to sit.

"Mnnnn," whined Dinah. She had sat and wouldn't get up. Everyone who didn't want to sit barked back.

Laughing, Mrs. Frank called, "Break time!"

The break gave Beau a chance to race outside and across the moist evening grass. He wet the flagpole and two bushes. Then he pulled Michael over to Dinah and her owner.

In just ten minutes, Beau was back in the gym again. But this time when Michael said, "Sit," Beau moved fast. He had to beat the bad collar.

Up went his head, down went his rump. He sat unmoving. And sure enough, the collar was good. It was quiet and it felt fine.

"Good dog!" cried Michael. "Hey, Debbie, watch this!"

Just then Mrs. Portly and Prudy pranced by. *Sassy, sassy,* went Prudy's bushy tail.

Beau stood and flattened his ears.

Prudy glared at him. "Yap, yap, yap!"

One swift move and he had that sassy tail in his mouth.

"NO!" hollered Michael, hauling on the leash.

"OOOOOOHHHHHH!" squealed Mrs. Portly, snatching Prudy away from Beau.

Beau happily spit out a few tail hairs.

"I warned you," Mrs. Frank called out as

she came over. "We cannot have fights. One more problem of any kind and you're out of the class."

Michael groaned. "Oh, man, now we're in big trouble."

8

At home, after school, Beau felt bad things in the air.

Dad's voice was loud. "You have to control him, Michael. Mrs. Frank can't teach if the dogs fight!"

"He has to behave," added Mom. "I won't live with a constant problem. I'll send him back to my brother."

"But, you guys, it isn't Beau's fault! I told you —"

Mom interrupted. "Can't we talk without yelling?"

"We're NOT YELLING!" Dad hollered.

Beau crept behind the draperies.

"You've scared the poor puppy," Mom said.

"Yeah!" said Michael. "Here, Beau, come on out."

Beau stayed where he was. Loud voices meant trouble, and they always hurt his ears.

"I'll put him out," Dad offered. "Sorry I yelled, but Beau must stay in that class. We can take turns going with him and that will make the teacher happy."

Dad picked Beau up, set him outside, and shut the door.

Beau felt awful. He moseyed over to a bush and wet it. No matter how he felt, it was important to keep his territory marked.

He went to the deep grassy place where he made three circles to the right, then two to the left. Just so. He sank down with an unhappy sigh.

"Ssss?" came from behind a far bush.

Beau's head jerked upward.

"SSSsssss." Louder this time.

He saw her now, her white tail whipping back and forth. It was the same fat, know-it-all cat. Just over the fence.

There she sat, unaware that he could jump the fence if he tried. He had once out-jumped his mother, long ago. The old life came sharply into mind.

He had always been free then. Chases had been common. Right now, he needed a chase and he itched to run free.

Beau backed up a few steps, aimed himself at the fence, and sailed over it.

"Yowww!" squawled the cat.

"Yowlp!" Beau replied joyously.

The cat led him up, around, right, and left — into the big park. He nearly had her tail in his mouth when she doubled back and scrambled up a tree.

From a high branch she gazed down. Her tail switched from side to side. She raised one paw and licked it, pretending he did not exist.

Beau panted below her. She had behaved just like a cat, cheating by running up a tree. He might have known cats would be the same no matter where they were.

Still, it had been a good chase. He turned to go home and soon discovered that he couldn't. He had no idea which way to go. The park was big and open and rolling, like his old home.

Of course, that home was far away. It would be a very long walk. But he remembered exactly how it had looked and smelled. Those were powerful memories.

And so he decided to go to a very high place and look for that home. From there, he'd know which way to go.

He headed west. Dusk became dark. In looking for a very high place, he trotted many hours into the night.

Near the edge of the city, he found a steep,

grassy hill. The grass comforted his feet, which were sore from the rough concrete.

Atop the hill he sat down and looked out to the west for a time. He turned north, his nose seeking clues. Then east, and south, and back to the west again.

Not one thing looked or smelled like his old home. And he was hungry and hurting.

He wanted Michael, and the good, soft bed, and the good, new food. That was the home he needed. *Right now* — not a long, painful walk away.

Whimpering, he looked east. Was it back that way? Or maybe to the north?

He couldn't find his new home, either.

Beau didn't know what to do. In the thin, dawn light, he threw back his head and howled for home.

9

Beau howled steadily. He gave it everything he had and so the sound traveled far.

Before long, an old Jack Russell terrier arrived.

Beau stood up as the Jack Russell came close.

The terrier nosed him all over, gently but thoroughly. When he turned to leave, Beau followed him.

Painfully, he limped down the hill after the Jack Russell. At the bottom of the hill, they went around to the back of a red-brick house.

"Rowf," sounded a retriever, loping across the backyard to meet them.

Beau yelped in surprise. This was the dog from school — the same friendly golden retriever.

Again, Beau stood still while he was inspected. The retriever gave his head one swift lick when she finished. Then she took the Jack Russell a short distance away, as if for a private talk.

Very soon, the terrier woofed a farewell and headed back toward the hill.

Beau lay down to lick his sore footpads. It seemed to him that he had been confused and lost for a very long time. He needed his new home and his boy and their bed.

"Rowf, rowf," the retriever urged, nudging Beau to his feet. She set off, looking back over her shoulder to make sure he followed.

Uncertain, Beau limped after her. He didn't know what else to do.

As dawn turned into day, across city blocks

and streets filling with traffic, the two dogs walked. Every now and then the retriever stopped until Beau caught up to her.

At those times, she gave his head a few strong, comforting licks. She was a strong dog altogether. She made him feel better, even though his feet were bleeding now from too many miles on concrete.

Beau had no idea where they were going. Hours ago, when he had left the park, he had thought only of finding a very high place. He had paid no attention to his route. He knew better now. He would never make that mistake again.

Finally, they turned a corner and Beau saw the high school. This was where he and the retriever had met!

The retriever looked back over her shoulder, her tongue lolling out. "See?" she seemed to say. "I can retrieve anything. It's my job, to fetch things and take them where they belong."

Together, the two dogs rested under a huge, yellow-leafed maple in front of the school. Beau licked his bloody feet and thought about home. He was close now, he was sure.

He gazed left, down a tree-shaded street. They had come to the school only twice, and always in the car. That made finding home harder.

But now he had hope. He rose to his feet, and the retriever followed.

Once he took them the wrong way, but in only a block he knew his mistake. Back they went, and Beau's nose told him the right way.

At last, Beau neared his own street. He recognized bushes and trees. He heard a dog bark that he had heard before. With a yelp of discovery, he picked up the pace.

He hobbled as fast as he could, right to the front door of his new home. He couldn't remember why he had left, but that, too, had been a mistake. He belonged here with the boy.

The retriever stayed only long enough to lick Beau's head. Then she was gone, back the way they had come.

10

Beau sat on the mat and barked. Never had he been this tired.

The door flew open.

"Beau!" all three people said at once.

Michael knelt and buried his face in Beau's neck. "Oh, Beau," he cried. "You came back!"

Dad picked Beau up and took him inside. They all sat on the sofa, with Beau across Michael's lap in the middle.

Mom started to kiss one paw. "Poor baby,

you must —" She broke off abruptly. "Uh-oh, look at his feet."

Dad winced. "I can't imagine how far he went — or how he ever found his way home. We covered every block for at least three miles."

"Let's feed him and take care of his feet and get some sleep," Mom suggested. "Good thing it's Saturday."

"Good thing he came home," Michael said.

Later, with a full stomach and bandaged paws, Beau settled next to Michael on the bed. He gave his boy's face a careful washing.

"Good dog," Michael whispered sleepily.

Beau's eyes closed. Now he could rest.

That afternoon, Beau lay in the grass and watched Michael and Dad work on the fence.

"Let's make it a lot higher," Dad suggested. "I think our dog is half kangaroo."

58

Mom came outside then. "The book on Bernese mountain dogs finally came. I'll read the interesting bits aloud while you guys work."

Beau ambled over to Mom and put his muzzle on her knee. He could count on her to stroke his head.

Her hand on his head, Mom read silently for a bit. Then she said, "Beau's ancestors went to Switzerland with Roman soldiers, ages ago. Bernese dogs still pull those big dairy carts in the Swiss mountains."

"Mmhmm," Dad said. "Hold that board steady, Michael."

"Pity we don't live on a ranch," Mom went on. "Then Beau could guard our homestead and herd our cattle —"

"Hey!" Michael dropped the board in his excitement. "That's just what the vet said! He needs *real jobs*."

"Pick up the board, Michael," Dad said.

Michael gazed into space. "If I got a paper

route, Beau could pull a cart for me. Wouldn't that be cool?"

"For cripes sake, Michael, pick up the board!"

Michael talked on. "Dad, you can build anything. If you made a cart, Beau and I could do all kinds of stuff. We could even get groceries. Okay, Dad?"

Dad put his hammer down. "Okay. I promise. Now please trade places with your mother. Janey?" he begged.

Mom laughed. "Here, Michael, you read."

Michael took the book and sat on the grass beside Beau. "This is what I wanted to do anyway," he said. He ran one hand through Beau's silky black coat.

Beau stretched out, his body touching Michael's. At peace, Beau felt himself dozing off. But before he let sleep come, he put one watchful paw on his boy's leg.

Other Springboard Books® You Will Enjoy, Now Available in Paperback: